# BEDDING THE BILLIONAIRE

## A TEMPERANCE FALLS ROMANCE

### LONDON HALE

# BEDDING THE *billionaire*

# LONDON HALE

LONDON HALE

*To our readers,*
*You are the chocolate to our peanut butter.*

# chapter one

## COLIN

THE FIRST WEEK Sloane had started working for me six months ago, she'd implemented weekly project reports on Monday mornings. She'd sit across from me, hair pulled back in a harsh ponytail, black-rimmed glasses perched on her nose, while reading details from her ever-present iPad. Which was exactly what she was doing now. Absolutely nothing was out of the ordinary.

Except the fact that I'd fucked her four times Saturday night, only to wake up to a cold, empty bed when I'd gone looking for round five.

Now she sat in the office at my estate, pretending none of it'd happened. Pretending I hadn't licked chocolate from her breasts, drunk champagne from the hollow of her stomach. That she hadn't screamed my name as I'd fucked her nearly off the bed. Then again in the shower. Then again bent over the kitchen counter. I'd fisted the hair now so perfectly styled and tugged until she'd looked back at me, begging me to fuck her deeper. And I had. As deep and hard as she'd wanted.

Yet here we were. Her giving me details for the coming week—all the while pretending the whole goddamn night never happened—as I sat behind my desk, hard as a fucking rock.

"The second floor's been opened to create the promenade effect, though we're waiting on a steel shipment to finalize the reinforcements and open what's to be the grand foyer. The Chinese manufacturer is difficult to deal with according to your local liaison, Frank, but they're our only option. I'm staying up on the order to make sure it's on the water in time."

Despite being sexy as hell when she was in business mode, her ignoring Saturday night pissed me off, though that irritation did nothing to deter my erection. Truthfully, I should've been thrilled at this outcome. Fucking a subordinate wasn't something I made a habit of—or did...ever—so I'd been strategizing since I'd found my bed empty, wondering what I'd need to do to keep her on this project.

Because there was no other option.

Sloane McLaren was the best at what she did, and I needed the best. Had offered her an exorbitant amount to get her ass on the island with me, too. In addition to her obscene paycheck, I covered her lodging at the local bed-and-breakfast, even though

I had a twelve-thousand-square-foot estate I'd never use even a quarter of. But it was worth it, because her reputation hadn't been exaggerated, and I needed the multimillion-dollar investment of the mixed-use facility to go off without a hitch.

And yet seeing her sitting there, all prim and proper and completely fucking professional, totally ignoring everything that'd happened between us, did nothing but make me want to mess her up. Undo her ponytail, take off those librarian-fantasy glasses, and ruck up her skirt. Bend her over the desk and lick her pussy. It did nothing but make me want her more. Which, to be honest, I hadn't thought possible.

"Exterior landscape design is finalized," she said, eyes still glued to her iPad. "I sent the sketches to you last night. We'll need to do some concrete work to accommodate the trees, which I've already scheduled for early spring so we stay on target."

I leaned back in my chair, twirling a pen between my fingers while she pretended I wasn't in the room. If I weren't paying attention, I would've missed the slight flush on her chest and the color pooling in her cheeks. Interesting. Seemed she wasn't quite as unaffected as she'd have me believe, considering she'd walked in at eight o'clock on the dot, calm as hell. She hadn't even given me a second glance. Just said good morning, took her typical seat at the chair in front of my desk, and dove into the reports.

I glanced down at the shirt she wore—light gray with a modest neckline—beneath her typical business suit. Absolutely nothing like what she'd worn to the holiday party on Saturday. Though, to be fair, she hadn't worn a shirt at all. Instead, she'd taken her office attire and turned it into the wardrobe for a CEO and subordinate porno—just a business jacket, buttoned right below her breasts. Practically serving them up on a platter. And I'd wanted nothing more than to have a taste.

"All I need is your approval on the parking garage refurbishment options, and we can get back to work. We're down to the final days before the holiday shutdown." She kept her eyes on her iPad, her fingers flying, always working. After long moments of silence, she finally looked up, her head cocked to the side. The first time she'd met my eyes all morning. "Colin? Are you listening?"

"I am." I studied her, holding her gaze so long she shifted in her seat. Finally, a crack in her facade. I could play it safe. Take the easy way out and not say anything, just thank my luck she'd shown up at all this morning. But I hadn't become a billionaire by thirty-four from playing it safe. "I'm just wondering how long you're going to continue with the meeting while pretending you didn't sit on my face over the weekend."

She let out a sharp cough and adjusted her glasses. "I didn't feel that particular...task needed a discussion. The fact that Chinese New Year is quickly approaching seemed far more vital to project completion."

"Yes, and you've done an excellent job keeping me abreast of the situation." My cell buzzed with an incoming call, and I dismissed it without glancing at the caller ID. "Is there anything else we need to go over?"

"No, I think we've covered everything."

"Good." I leaned forward, bracing my elbows on my desk. "Then we can discuss why you ran out in the middle of the night without a word."

She straightened her shoulders, her jaw ticking once—the only sign of her irritation. "I don't think that's a good idea. There's a lot of work to do to keep this project on schedule, and neither of us needs distractions. Let's call it what it was—a lapse in judgment—and move on."

Bullshit. She was completely full of bullshit. It was almost insulting she thought I'd fall for it, considering how closely we'd been working together for the past six months. I could smell a lie a mile away, and she certainly didn't have the poker face to try to slip one past me. She wanted me, wanted more of what we'd done over the weekend. She just didn't think she should.

So I pushed. "Which time, exactly, would you call the lapse in judgment—when I fucked you in the kitchen or the shower?"

The flush on her cheeks and chest grew, and she darted her eyes away, but not before letting her gaze drop to my lips. "I believe we could go all the way back to the second bottle of champagne."

My eyebrows shot up. I didn't recall her being drunk on Saturday—if she had been, I'd never have taken her to bed. Tipsy, yes. Relaxed enough to slip out of Business Sloane mode? Hell yes. But drunk? "Are you saying you were too intoxicated to realize what you were doing?"

She shook her head before I'd gotten all the words out. "Not at all. But partaking of that bottle was a mistake considering…"

"Considering the fact that I'm your boss?"

"Considering the mess we're finding ourselves in," she said, harsher. The tone I referred to as her pit-bull voice—the one she used when dealing with vendors and contractors. The one that said she took no shit.

Too bad.

"I think you've worked with me long enough to know I don't do lapses in judgment. Nor do I believe in regrets, and I rarely make mistakes. So I'm going to have to disagree with you. I think the second bottle was the perfect ending to the night." I cocked my head to the side and met her eyes. "Or the perfect start to it, anyway."

Her fingernail tapped her iPad screen, something she did when she was nervous or uncertain. Like I said, no poker face. She was an open book, if one was to look close enough. "Colin, I work for you, and we have a very big job ahead of us that could cost you millions and me my career if anything goes south. What happened over the weekend needs to stay in the weekend."

I studied her for long moments, taking in the stiff line of her shoulders and the set of her jaw. Sloane tended to reach a point when she'd had enough. I'd seen it happen in countless meetings. She was definitely there now. Time to pull back and reconsider my options.

With a short nod, I conceded. "I'll drop it"—for now—"if you tell me one thing… Do you want to forget about the weekend because you don't want it to happen again, or because you don't think you should?"

She froze, her entire body going stiff as she locked her eyes on mine. "I'm not sure the difference is important."

"I see." I tapped my pen twice on my desk. Getting her back in my bed was going to be a challenge, but I'd never been one to shy away from them. "If that's all, then?"

Her mouth dropped open, and she blinked before seeming to snap herself out of it. "Yes. That's all."

"Good. Will you be in your office the rest of the day, or on-site?"

"I'll be on-site until lunch but will close out the day here."

I gave a brief nod and picked up my phone, using the time to pretend I was checking the calls and emails I'd missed during the meeting—something I always did once our weekly progress reports were winding down. In actuality, I was using the time to plan. "I was hoping you'd say that. I'd like to make a trip there today, as well." I glanced at her. "We can ride over together."

Her lips pressed together in a poor imitation of a smile. "Of course. I was planning to leave on the hour."

"I'll have George ready." I shot a quick message to my driver, letting him know to have the car around front in twenty minutes. Time to play hardball. "I'll also want a detailed inventory of the expected shipment on my desk before you leave for the evening."

Her lips pulled down at the corners, her brow creased. "Those numbers come from China. It'll be quite late before I have access to them."

That worked just fine for me. "Then I guess it's going to be a long night."

She nodded stiffly. "Whatever you need." She clutched her iPad to her chest as she stood. "If that's all?"

With a nod from me, she took her cue and turned to leave, her ass swaying more than usual. Goddamn, that ass. Shapely, round, and perfectly fucking biteable. And I had, too—spanked it and bit it and dug my fingers into it as I'd taken her from behind.

My cock ached, but I wasn't going to get relief anytime soon. I had an unplanned trip to the project site this morning and arrangements to be made for tonight.

One of the things that made Sloane excel at her job was her straightforward approach, which was why her reaction threw me. She gave off all kinds of signals, and I needed to figure out which were the genuine reflection of her desires. If she truly didn't want anything more to happen between us, that'd be that. I'd respect her wishes and continue on as if the best sex of my life didn't reside between those shapely legs of hers.

But if she did want it? That was a different story entirely. And fortunately, I wasn't one known for giving up.

# chapter two

SLOANE

"ARROGANT, ANNOYING MAN." I slammed my iPad down before walking around the corner of my desk and plopping into my chair, thankful Colin worked at the opposite end of the hall so he wouldn't hear me. God forbid I piss off the domineering, overbearing jackass who paid my salary. And made my panties wet.

Colin Huntley had appeared on my radar screen as nothing more than a name in a news article while I'd been working toward my MBA. He had enough money to finance the projects I preferred—large-scale, huge-budget, tight-deadline. I'd worked my way up through the ranks of bank projects, corporate builds, then into the elite world of billionaire real estate. I wanted those projects, the ones I needed to make my dreams of retiring early a reality. But chasing my entrepreneurial vision had always come at a cost. I was paid well for my skills, sure, but also for my ability to live anywhere, anytime, for however long it took. I had no home, no roots, and no commitments other than my job. Need me to go to China immediately? My passport was in my purse. Want me in Brazil for a year to make sure the latest resort gets finished on budget? I could be packed in five minutes.

Need me to move to an island in the Midwest for six months, including the holiday season, to run a project turning an old shopping mall into something else? Easy. Until him.

When my phone rang, I swiped to answer without looking at the screen. "Sloane McLaren."

"Sloane McLaren, Colin Huntley. Just wanted to let you know we're set to leave in five."

I glanced at the clock, my brow tightening when I saw the time. "Yes. That was the plan, sir."

"You know I like to give adequate prep time." He paused, the silence weighted, his voice dropping when he finally spoke again. "To make sure you're ready for me."

Sweet Jesus. My hand shook as I disconnected the call. If I thought banging my head against my desk would help stave off the need to both slap and kiss that man's face, I would've done it. How had I gotten myself into this mess? I was a professional— an educated, independent, successful woman. I didn't submit to men like Colin Huntley. I stood up to them, led them down the path of my choosing, and directed their actions. I didn't lust after them, and I certainly didn't sleep with them. Multiple times. So much so that I'd walked with a slight limp the next morning. I knew better.

Or at least I had until I'd actually met Colin.

For all the research I'd conducted on his business, I'd missed looking into his personal life. I was used to working with rich, elderly men sporting big bellies and almost no hair. I hadn't been prepared for Colin to be so goddamned attractive. The man exuded something that made my brain go fuzzy and my knees weaken. The first time his hazel eyes had met mine, I'd almost stopped breathing. The instant arousal that look had initiated had been something new, something unique. Something I had to ignore.

But ignoring Colin was…difficult, to say the least. He was fit, muscular even, with constant scruff and a face that had women throwing themselves at him. His wallet seemed just as interesting to them. He dated supermodels and A-list actresses. I was neither of those by a long shot. That wasn't to say I wasn't attractive—I knew my body was tight and my face got attention. I wasn't a supermodel, though. I was Colin's employee. I'd assumed my lusting after him would go unnoticed if I kept myself in check. I'd hoped, at least.

And then came the party.

I'd thought I was winning the battle against his sex appeal. I gave him updates every morning, ignoring his hazel eyes and his dark hair just long enough to make a girl want to hold on and ride that scruffy chin of his. I didn't breathe too heavily, whimper when he ran his thumb along his lower lip, or giggle at everything he said.

Craving a distraction, I pulled up my email, needing to clear my head of Colin and his sex hair before I soaked my lace panties. I had too much work to do, and apparently, part of that was a car ride over to the construction site with the boss. The same boss I'd worn the panties for. Not that he'd ever know. It wasn't like we were going to discuss Saturday night. The way he'd stripped me down so roughly before kissing his way up my legs. How he'd spoken the filthiest words while gently running his hands over my body. How solid and thick he was as he'd pushed inside. As he'd fucked me every which way and left me begging for more.

One slip of concentration, and I'd fallen prey to the most infuriating man I'd ever met. I had a feeling that wouldn't be the only time if I didn't stay far away from him.

"George has the car around front," Colin said as he leaned inside the doorway. Of course. I needed distance, and he intended to discuss groin arches and grout thickness. Which only made me think about his thickness. That heavy, delicious cock that had filled me so well.

"Sloane?"

Shit…focus.

"Sorry." I shook my head to clear it. "I'm ready

to go." I rose from my chair and reached for my iPad. My hand trembled, and my chest felt warmer than normal. Both things I needed to keep him from noticing. "Should I call Ted to make sure he's available for lunch?"

"Not necessary. He won't be joining us."

Danger, Will Robinson. "Okay, so we'll skip—"

"We'll still be going to lunch."

"Just the two of us?"

"Yes."

Oh no. No, no, no. I racked my brain, trying to think of something to keep this time professional. "Let me grab my spreadsheets. We can go over the import landing costs. Will you need anything specific while we're there?"

His eyes locked on mine, almost seeming to grow darker. Heated. I knew that look, had practically felt it Saturday night. That was the look of Colin when he needed something, all right. But I doubted cost analysis and demographic updates would satiate him.

"Oh, definitely. But I'm not sure what I have in mind would be appropriate with all the construction workers around."

Yeah, my spreadsheets weren't going to save me.

---

And so the week went. Every day, Colin found some way to end up at lunch together or keep me late so he could talk to me alone. I didn't know how he managed it, but he even had other people involved. On Wednesday, he'd made dinner plans for us with the mayor of Temperance Falls and her new husband. They hadn't shown up. Not canceled or notified us to reschedule. They simply never came to the restaurant. I'd ended up stuck across from Colin for two hours all alone.

Though stuck wasn't the word I'd use, if I was being honest. Colin was…funny. Charming, as I'd expected, but kind and thoughtful outside the office. He still demanded and overwhelmed people, but there was something relaxed about him when we were alone. Something almost sweet in how he took care of me.

I could not surrender to his seductions again, though.

"Anything I can get you before I leave, Ms. McLaren?" Emery, the local woman Colin had hired as his personal assistant, stood at the doorway to my office, carrying her coat and purse. I couldn't blame her for wanting to leave. The holidays were almost upon us, and we were dropping down to a skeleton crew for the next week or so. A skeleton crew consisting mostly of Colin and me. Alone.

"I'm fine, Emery, but thank you. Have a lovely holiday."

With a nod, she hurried off, leaving me alone in

Colin's Temperance Falls mansion. I hadn't seen him all day, a fact that seemed odd after the past week of him constantly in my face. Maybe he'd been busy. Or maybe, just maybe, he'd gotten sick of chasing me. I couldn't blame him. I'd been downright frosty, fighting hard to keep the professional barrier in place. It'd exhausted me and left me feeling a little… lonely.

I fingered the little pine tree someone had set up on the corner of my desk, wishing I had somewhere to go. That I had holiday plans. That I had someone to spend an evening under a big Christmas tree with. "Bah fucking humbug."

"I never took you for a Scrooge."

I jerked back, my eyes meeting Colin's almost out of instinct. He leaned against the doorjamb, his shirt unbuttoned under his suit vest, tie loose. Casual. And oh-so-very hot.

"Colin." I coughed once, trying to kill the breathy, fuck-me-now voice that had snuck into my throat. "I assumed you'd gone to the residence wing already."

"Now why would I do that when you're still here?" He pushed off the wall, positively swaggering toward me. So presumptuous. So fucking arrogant. "Besides, it's late, and you haven't eaten. I had Clara prepare lasagna for us."

Oh no. That was…unfair wasn't a strong enough word. He knew I loved lasagna—had listened as I'd regaled him with stories of what I'd done to get it no matter where I was in the world. I couldn't resist it. I'd just have to resist him.

"That was awfully presumptuous of you. I might have plans."

A single flicker of doubt danced across his too-handsome face. "Do you?"

I wanted to say yes. Wanted it so badly, the lie sat on the tip of my tongue like a weight. But I couldn't lie to Colin, not really. Not like that. "No. I don't."

"Then it looks like we'll be enjoying a nice dinner together." His grin turned mischievous in a way that made me think he knew exactly how this would go. The bastard. "I think I'll have a bottle of champagne chilling, too."

He darted a look down to my stomach, probably remembering the same thing I was. His tongue on my skin as he'd lapped champagne off me last weekend. The weekend of my huge fail in keeping a professional boundary between us. That look was not an invitation—it was an assumption. One that pivoted my psyche from turned on to pissed off. "This is getting ridiculous, Colin. You can't keep playing these games to steal time with me. I'm here as your employee, not your girlfriend."

He didn't even blink at my raised voice. "Tell me, Sloane, have you had a terrible time this week?"

"That doesn't matter."

His chuckle made the fire in my blood burn hotter. "That's answer enough." He edged around the corner of my desk, spinning my chair so we faced one another, then leaned over to box me in. "And if you really wanted me to stop, why have you changed your patterns this week?"

Jesus, his eyes were just so…pretty. "I have no idea what you're talking about."

"No? You think I don't notice when you wear something out of the ordinary? Or keep your hair down more? Or put on that hot-as-fuck red lipstick you know drives me insane?" He glanced down, brushing a finger across my bottom lip. "You know exactly what that does to me. I told you while you had my dick between those pretty red lips."

Yes. Yes, he had. He'd dropped a lot of filthy words and promises that night. But this was different, this was over the line. This was…too tempting to resist. I smacked his hand away and rose to my feet. "You don't get to say such things to me."

Colin stepped closer, herding me back until my ass hit the bookshelf next to the window behind my desk. Trapping me in a way that made me tremble with anticipation, not fear. "If you can tell me right now you haven't enjoyed every second of this week, haven't gotten yourself off to memories of Saturday night, I'll walk away. We won't ever speak of it again."

I opened my mouth to refute him but closed it again. I couldn't find the words to lie. Truth was, I'd enjoyed my time with him. Outside of the office, he was the sort of guy I'd be interested in. But we had to work together, and Office Colin was a dick. A thought that only made me think of his dick…again.

I'd dreamed of it, gotten myself off a number of times to the memory of what this man could do to my body. Hell, I'd come twice this morning remembering the feel of him on top of me.

Which was so not what I needed to be thinking about.

"You're an asshole, you know that?"

Colin's lips quirked again, that knowing look back. He was even daring enough to run a finger along my collarbone and over my cleavage. A featherlight touch that set my skin ablaze.

"Is that a no?" He stepped closer, brushing his body against mine, completely overwhelming my senses. "Because if not, I'm going to slide my fingers under that tight skirt and see if you're as wet as I think you are." He leaned forward, his lips against my ear, the weight of his chest pinning me in place. "And you're going to let me."

I gasped, the feel of him so close turning my knees to rubber and soaking my panties. His lips were on mine in a flash in what I could only describe as a brutal kiss. I thrust my tongue against his, trying to take control, but he was bigger. Stronger. He shoved me against the bookcase and grabbed my face between his palms. Controlling me. The jackass.

"God, I hate you sometimes," I said when he moved his lips down to my neck.

He bit down hard, making me jump as he grabbed my thigh. "But not all the time. You don't hate me when you're screaming my name."

True, though I wasn't ready to admit that. I wanted to fight instead. But his fingers were inching under my skirt, and his lips and tongue were working their magic on my throat. The man was lust in human form, sensual and sexual at once. Too tempting to say no to, and too fucking hot for his own good.

"Come on, spitfire. Spread these beautiful legs, and let me see what's waiting for me."

I groaned, giving in to my desire and doing as he asked. I wasn't fully surrendering, though. Not really. It was more…a break. A moment of peace in the middle of the fight. I could hate him again once he'd fucked me six ways to Sunday. I needed him to make me come, wanted him so badly, I couldn't resist.

I grabbed hold of his shoulders as he tugged my panties aside to run his knuckle through my slit. Once, twice…he teased with a light pressure, rubbing back and forth as he stared down at me. Looking as if he was waiting for something. Holding out on me.

I wasn't having that. "You might as well stop now if you're not going to get me off."

The grin was back, the one that said he saw through me, and he kept up his maddeningly slow pace. "Ah, but you don't want me to stop, do you? Maybe I should tease you and make you wait, just like you've done to me this week. Get you right to the point of coming all over me, then pull back… Or maybe not."

"Fuck," I yelped, my body arching toward him as he plunged his fingers inside of me. Two, three…I had no idea, but I felt full. Complete. Ready to come. He pressed his thumb against my clit and pumped in and out, fucking me roughly with his hand.

"I think we both know I love watching you come too much to do that. Love how this pussy squeezes my fingers and cock, don't I?" He leaned in, taking my bottom lip between his and giving it a solid suck before releasing. "Now give me room to work. Pull that skirt up so I can see how wet you've made my hand."

Shameless, I yanked up my skirt over my hips and spread my legs wider, even going so far as to set my right foot on a shelf to give him more room. If I was going to dance with the devil again, I might as well make it more than just a middle-school sway. And Colin was nothing if not a little on the devilish side.

It didn't take long for him to have me melted against him, writhing on his hand. "So good. I'm gonna…I'm close."

"You're close because I'm working over this pussy perfectly, aren't I? Less than twelve hours spent between your legs, and I already know exactly what it takes to get you off."

"Just shut up and make me come."

His hand disappeared, the emptiness left behind stealing my breath. For one moment, for one brief, hanging-over-the-edge second, I honestly thought I'd pushed him too far. That he was leaving me like this—wet, swollen, so fucking wanting.

I should've known he'd never surrender.

Without warning, his fingers snapped forward, smacking my pussy with a popping sound. "That's not how we ask nicely."

I jerked, unable to hold still as a shot of pleasure-laced pain stormed through me. The man was a beast, an animal, unable to be tamed. And though it was fun to try, I was over waiting. I needed him. Wanted him. So I gave a little.

"Please," I whispered. "Is that nice enough for you?"

His soft laugh pissed me off, but it also pushed me right over the edge along with the extra deep thrust of his fingers inside me. I came with a loud moan, pulling Colin closer and stealing a passionate kiss from him as I clenched and shook. Fuck, he was so good at this. So good at everything. It was an annoying gift for the man to have, but at that moment, I was nothing but grateful.

At least until he opened his mouth again.

"You know the only time you quit fighting is when you're coming all over me?" He took his hand away, bringing his fingers to his mouth so he could lick them clean. How anything so filthy was so hot, I had no idea. But it was. As was his cocky arrogance as he said, "Hope you're ready for round two."

# chapter three

COLIN

THIS WOMAN GOT ME every fucking time. There was something about the glint of challenge in her eyes that made me hard as granite. Something about the way she pushed back instead of rolling over that had me wanting to devour her. All week, she'd pretended to be put out by my plans, to be inconvenienced when she'd enjoyed a five-star dinner and a thousand-dollar bottle of wine with me. But that fire had never reached her eyes—if it had, I would've quit.

Instead, she'd waved a red flag in front of a bull, playing games, same as I'd done to her. Since I'd confronted her, she'd kept her hair loose instead of pulling it back in her signature ponytail—which, of course, had only reminded me of when I'd had the locks spread out on my pillow. And then on Tuesday—and every day thereafter—she'd worn flaming red lipstick. The exact color she'd left in a ring around my cock Saturday night. She'd put a little more sway into her hips when she'd walked, and she'd even begun to anticipate our dinner plans, her office light still burning well after she'd normally have left for the day.

But Sloane would never dream of entering a relationship—sexual or otherwise—with her boss, because she was the kind of woman who lived by the rules.

Fortunately, I was the kind of man who broke them.

"Open my pants and take out my cock."

"Maybe I'm not in the mood to take orders from you. Besides, I'd rather ride your face again."

"The next time you come, it's going to be on my cock." I stepped into her, letting her feel the hard ridge of my erection against her stomach. Letting her feel exactly how much I wanted her. "And we both know you're desperate to come again, so there's no need to be coy. You've got a greedy little pussy, don't you?"

Truth be told, I was the one who was desperate to come, but I'd hold out. If I had to jack it in the shower to thoughts of her coming all over my fingers, I would. But I would not be the one opening my pants tonight. I needed that from her…needed her to show me she wanted this as badly as I did, needed her acquiescence. She might not like that she wanted this thing between us, but I was tired of her denying it.

"Fine." She slid her fingers into the waistband of my suit pants and jerked me closer before unfastening my belt and pants. "If you want my hands, you can have them."

I wanted to spout off some smartass remark about her finally seeing it my way, but her hand wrapped around my cock stole every word. All I could do was groan into her neck, my hips thrusting forward of their own accord. "Hasn't even been a week, and I've missed your hands on me."

"If you think my hands feel good, wait until you slide inside me. I've been wet for you for days."

Before she could make me come in her hand like a goddamn teenager, I pulled out of her grip and spun her to the side, caging her against the window. She rested her hands on either side of her head on the glass, her face turned to the side and looking back at me. Lips swollen, ass upturned, and glistening pussy peeking out from between her spread legs, she was a fucking wet dream come to life.

"How'd I go six months?" The question was more to me than her, whispered under my breath as I sheathed my cock with a condom and once again pressed against her back. After this week of abstaining, it was a goddamn miracle I'd been able to do it the first six months of her employment with me. I had absolutely no desire to go back to that. Not after I'd had her.

I slid the tip of my cock through her slit, spreading her wetness, rubbing circles around her clit.

Shuddering, she lifted her ass a little more, offering her pussy to me. Just how I wanted it. "You ready for me?"

"Yes." She reached back, digging her fingernails into my leg, but my damn pants got in the way. We hadn't even stopped long enough to unbutton her shirt or take off my vest, simply removing the necessary articles that stood in the way of me getting inside her. That was what happened when we'd denied ourselves for nearly a week. Combustion.

But next time? Next time, I was going to spend an hour licking her pussy. She'd be naked and spread out on my bed before the evening was through.

I brought my cock to her entrance, letting the tip rest there without pushing inside. "Tell me how much you want it."

"So your ego can get stroked a little more at my expense? No thank you," she said, even as she lifted on her tiptoes and tilted her hips back, chasing my cock.

"Admitting you want me doesn't make you weak. God knows I want this pussy." I finally put us both out of our misery, pushing into her and sliding deep in one swift thrust. "Christ, I'm a starving man for it, aren't I?"

"Then fuck me like you are."

With a growl, I gripped her hair in my fist, tugging her head back and exposing her neck. I nipped the delicate skin as I pumped into her without restraint. We could go slow later. Hell, I'd take her slow five times tonight if she wanted. Right now, I was desperate for her. Desperate to feel her come apart on my cock, desperate to feel her body go pliant against mine. There was something gratifying in knowing I could make this tough-as-nails woman soften even for a moment, all because of what I did to her.

"Deeper… Colin, fuck me harder." She lifted her ass, trying to get as much of me inside her as possible. Arched back, fingers clawing at the glass, panting breaths against my neck…this fierce woman was reduced to pure need.

And I was more than willing to give her what she wanted.

I gripped her under one knee, bringing it up to rest against the window and opening her to take my cock all the way. Opening her enough that anyone who was looking from outside could see exactly what we were doing. Despite the grounds surrounding the estate being vacant, the idea of someone witnessing this only made me hotter. Had me pumping into her harder and faster as I thought of people seeing who was bringing this powerhouse of a woman pleasure enough that she surrendered.

"You didn't need to tell me that. I know exactly what this pussy needs." I slipped my other hand around her hip and straight down between her legs, not stopping until I circled her clit. Her fingers curled against the glass, her head resting back against my shoulder, mouth hanging open in silent pleasure. "You want every single inch I've got stuffed inside this tight little heaven, isn't that right? Deep and hard. I remember. I remember exactly what you need."

She reached down, gripping my forearm as I teased her clit, her nails digging into my skin. One of the signs she was close. One of the signs she needed me to go faster and harder. I pinched her clit between my fingers and slammed into her from behind, pumping into her in a frenzied rhythm.

"See? Knew you needed me to work this clit faster. Knew you needed me to get a little rough." I scraped my teeth against her neck, then bit down as her back bowed, her blouse-covered breasts pressed against the window. "I know just what to do to have this pussy coming all over me, don't I?"

"Oh God, I'm—" She broke off on a loud moan, thrusting her hips back to meet mine. Her pussy squeezed my cock as she came, my name a panted chant on her lips.

That was all it took for me to surrender. With my lips pressed to her neck, I thrust as deep as I could and let go, my orgasm overwhelming me as I spilled inside her.

As soon as our breathing evened out, I gripped my cock and pulled out, discarding the condom and grabbing a couple tissues from Sloane's desk. She stood still, resting against the window, her breaths puffing steam clouds on the glass, skirt rucked up around her waist. Sloane McLaren's perfect facade sullied—by me.

After cleaning her up, I tossed the tissues and

righted her skirt—pity, but I'd be seeing that fine ass bent over my bed in about five minutes—before tucking myself in my pants, ready to guide her straight to my bedroom.

She turned around, smoothing her skirt, her professional mask slipping on as if I hadn't just fucked her up against the window in her office. "I'm sure you have other things to do. I should probably head out."

I stepped closer, lifting her chin with my fingers. "C'mon, spitfire, you know me better than that. This was just an appetizer. You think I'd let you spend the night anywhere but my bed?" Slipping my hand down to her neck, I wrapped my fingers around her nape and bent to brush my lips against hers. "It's been almost a week since I've been tongue deep in your pussy, and I plan to rectify that tonight."

# chapter four



I WOKE SLOWLY, THE morning light barely making it past the heavy curtains across from me. Curtains that didn't match the decor of my room at the local B&B. It took a second for my memories to catch up with me, for the aches in my muscles to make sense, but when they did…

"Stay with me, spitfire. I want you next to me when I wake up."

Right. Colin. For a brief moment, I smiled and snuggled deeper into the heavy blankets over me and the strong man at my back. Colin had worn me out the night before, working me over for hours in positions I hadn't even known existed. He'd had me riding his face before we even made it all the way to his bedroom, then had flipped me up into his arms and carried me right to his bed. On top, behind, underneath, sideways—the man was a sexual gymnast, and I'd honestly worried I wouldn't be able to keep up. But I did, and it was so worth the way my body hurt from the exertion.

But he was still Colin—still my boss—and still an asshole at times. Plus, we would most certainly have work to do. Hell, my phone was probably already ringing and my email box filled. We also had a huge conference call later we needed to focus on. Time to throw the professional barrier back up. Which meant getting out of bed and putting clothes on. Soon. Maybe in a few minutes. If I could only—

"Stop it." Colin pulled me closer and nuzzled the back of my neck. "I can hear you thinking. Quit trying to talk yourself out of staying in bed with me."

I hated when he was so...smart. "We should be working already."

He slipped his hand between my legs, opening me for him. Pulling me until he could rock his hips and have his heavy cock slide against where I was already sore from him. Where I felt as if I'd never get enough of him.

"Colin." My voice was a warning, a threat. One he definitely didn't take seriously. He chuckled against my neck and rolled me onto my stomach, laying his entire weight along the length of me and using one hand to line himself up. I wanted to argue, to tell him we had too many things to do, but I couldn't. I simply could not find the words to refuse him when he was so close. So I inched my legs apart as far as I could and tilted my hips to take him inside.

"See? Greedy little pussy, and I fucking love it." He nipped at my ear, his touch soft and his voice gentle. "You're not too sore?"

"Not for this, no." I groaned as he pushed in deep, definitely sore but knowing he was about to make everything worthwhile. The man filled me so well, always seemed to know exactly what I wanted and how to give it to me. There was no denying we worked together physically. On any other level, though, I had my doubts. But for the moment, I could give myself over to him. Let him push me down into the mattress and take what he wanted as he gave me everything I needed. I'd go back to hating him later.

Much, much later.

"Oh God." I fisted the sheets and bit my lip, trying so hard not to come just yet. It was damn near embarrassing how quickly Colin could get me off. How easy I was for him. How sloppy he made me with just his words. But there was no holding back with him. No resisting.

He pushed forward and bit down on my neck, marking me again as he had numerous times overnight. I probably looked as if I'd been in bed with a vampire, but I didn't care. At that moment, with him totally in control of my body, I let go. I gave myself over to the pleasure he worked out of me and fell, clenching around him. Shaking and twitching as every synapse in my body fired at once.

Colin grunted and pressed deep one last time, coming with a groan that only made me want him more. "Jesus, can't last when this pussy squeezes me so perfectly, can I? Fucking heaven…"

It took me several seconds to catch my breath, long enough for Colin to give my shoulder a sweet kiss before rolling off me to get up and take care of the condom I didn't remember him putting on. Always so detail oriented, my Colin.

No. Not my. Never my.

"I'll have Clara prepare us breakfast." He strolled out of the bathroom. Completely naked, completely casual. As if walking around in front of me with no clothes on was normal. "She can make you anything in the world, but I have a feeling you're going to tell me to order you yogurt and granola."

"Yes, please." I rolled over, taking the sheet with me, suddenly uncomfortable. He knew what I liked to have for breakfast every day. He paid attention to me. That didn't quite fit the Colin in my head. The one I worked with, the one who seemed to care only about himself. But Colin had proven he didn't just care about himself. He was a giving partner in bed, skilled and patient. He certainly seemed to enjoy what he did to me, and I definitely enjoyed the attention. But fitting Colin the lover and Colin the boss together into one was too much for me to handle without caffeine in my system. "Coffee would be nice as well."

He popped out of his closet, suit in hand. "Already

brewing in the sitting area. Why don't you head into the shower? After I call down to get breakfast started, I'll join you." He shot me a mischievous grin as he laid the navy garment that probably cost more than an average car over the chair. "How many times do you think I can make you come before the food arrives?"

"Presumptuous again." I gave him the best glare I could muster, which really wasn't much of one. I was too blissed out on all the sex, too warm and sated. And too turned on by thoughts of him fucking me against the shower walls again to care. "Maybe I'd like to shower alone."

"Maybe I'd like you to ride my tongue."

The man definitely knew how to drive a bargain. "Fine. Meet you in there in five."

"Three." He smacked my ass as I slipped past him. "And not a second longer."

———

"I want to get to the manufacturing schedule," Colin said, looking so damn handsome as he read the report I'd just slid across his desk. "But first, how about you tell me why the quality assurance tests are coming back with failures on tensile strength?"

The man on the other end of the line—Frank, Colin's local contact in Shanghai—started spouting off about our standards and the limitations of steel manufacturing. All things we'd heard before. Still, we'd been promised multiple containers of specific pieces we needed to safely support the second-level balconies in the mall revamp project. Pieces we no longer had time to source domestically. Without the shipment, our project came to a halt. That couldn't happen.

"I'm tired of the excuses, Frank." Colin ran a hand over his head. "Do I need to send my Operations VP over there to get this done on time? Because I will. Ms. McLaren is sitting right here, and I'm sure she'd have no problem catching the red-eye."

"Absolutely." I leaned closer to the speaker. "I can be there tomorrow if need be. And I'll take over the negotiations with the factories. Just give me the word, sir."

Colin raised an eyebrow, giving me a smile that seemed almost wicked as he pushed the mute button. "I love it when you call me sir. Have I told you that?"

Damn him. It'd been hours since we'd left his bedroom, far too long since he'd made me come. He'd kissed me multiple times since then, had snuck into my office twice to hitch up my skirt and tease me right to the edge before leaving me wet and wanting. The man was trying to seduce me, to get me to make the first move.

And he was winning.

"No, you haven't, sir." I leaned forward, running a hand along my collarbone to draw his attention lower. "But I may have noticed a particular physical reaction you have when I do it. One that definitely showed your approval."

"Have you now?" He pushed back from the desk, holding out one arm to me. "Care to see if I'm having that reaction now?"

"We're on a call."

"I'm the CEO. I can end it." He reached for the phone, but I shook my head.

"Don't." I'd never been any sort of exhibitionist—never cared for anyone to see into the bedroom of my partner and me. But I'd spent six months denying my attraction to this man. Six long months of sitting across from him and listening to him command a call or dominate another employee. Hell, he'd dominated me, and knowing him as I did now? I liked it. And I didn't want to wait another minute to show him.

Without giving myself too much time to think about what I was about to do, I bit my lip and slipped around the desk, only half listening to the other people on the call go back and forth about expectations and limitations. For once in my life, work would have to wait. I had a staff of people who could fill me in, and it was about time I utilized them. Right at that moment, I had an urge to do something to Colin. To have that man at my mercy.

He had definitely won the seduction game.

"You were cruel this morning when you teased me right to the edge and didn't make me come."

"Was I?"

"Yes. Definitely." I pushed his shoulder, forcing

his chair back, giving myself room to work. "I wore your favorite lipstick today."

"I noticed." He reached up, running his thumb over my bottom lip. I flicked my tongue against the tip, giving him a preview of what I had in store.

"It'll leave a mark if I kiss you." I dropped to my knees, unfastening his pants with a smile on my face. "Or do more than just kiss you."

"I'm hoping for it." His voice was deep, almost growly, and his eyes were bright as they held mine. This was a man who wanted, one who craved whatever I was promising. And that fact, knowing I could push him to the point of looking at me like I was a gift to him, made me feel far more powerful than sitting across from him in my suit ever had.

"I'd dream of this sometimes," I said as I pulled his cock through the placket of his pants. "When we were on a conference call and there were people waiting for us to direct them. I would think about what it'd be like to slip under your desk and take you in my mouth."

Colin ran his finger down the side of my cheek, breathing hard. Silent. But there was a tension about him. An energy that said he was ready to go off. And I couldn't wait to be the one to make him.

I opened my mouth and ran my tongue around the head of his cock, staring into his eyes. Flicking the slit twice before placing a big, wet kiss to the tip. "I wonder if I can make the powerful Colin Huntley beg."

He chuckled deeply, sighing as I wrapped my lips around the tip again and sucked. "I don't beg, spitfire, but I'd beg for these lips around my cock. Every fucking night."

I popped off him, licking the tip once more. "Someday, I'm going to make you prove it."

But today was not that day. I was too wired, too worked up. Instead of waiting for him to beg, I opened my mouth and slid him between my lips. Colin's hand came to rest on the side of my face, his fingers slipping into my hair as his thumb caressed the corner of my mouth. So gentle. So sweet. So fucking filthy.

"Jesus Christ, do you know what the sight of you does to me?" he asked as he wrapped a hand in my hair and began to direct my movements. "On your knees in my office, pretty red lips spread tight around my cock?"

I hummed, rocking my body and swallowing around him. Trying to take him deeper. Trying to make him lose control. His groans became a long litany of curse words, his hand on my face more a directional force than a simple touch.

"Fuck, you suck me so good. Can't decide which I love more—your mouth or your sweet pussy."

Good goddamn, I was wet. Between the taste of him on my tongue, the fact that I could still hear the other people talking on the call, and the way his hands gripped me tight then relaxed to run softly against my cheeks before grasping me again, I was close to coming. No one had ever gotten me so worked up, no man's surrender to this act had ever sent me close to my own release so fast. But this wasn't just anyone. This was Colin Huntley, billionaire real estate mogul, dater of supermodels, and my boss. Those facts ramped up the hotness to the nth degree.

It was on a particularly deep pull from me, as one of the men on the call said my name, that he finally broke. "That's it, spitfire. I need to be inside you."

I sucked all the way to the end of him, keeping my hand stroking his length as I kissed the tip once. Twice. "I'm already soaked for you, but I'm not sure I can come listening to Frank talk about ore components."

Colin's arm shot out, his hand nearly knocking the phone off the desk before finding the right button.

"Great work, team," Colin said, his voice only moderately strained. "I'm going to have to drop off. Figure this out and update Ms. McLaren and me within the hour."

He slammed his finger on the disconnect button then groaned and lifted me right off the ground with barely more than a grunt. His hands were rough as he tossed me on his desk, his movements harried as he stripped off my panties and slid two fingers inside of me. "Jesus, you weren't lying. Just sucking me off gets your pussy dripping, doesn't it?"

"I told you I'd dreamt of doing that." I spread my legs around his hips and pulled him tighter, not giving him a chance to reach for the condom I knew he had in his wallet. "We can do this bare. I'm safe and on the pill." I reached between us, stroking his length. Tugging him closer. "I want to feel you."

He froze, body locked in place, cock growing harder in my hands as he stared down at me with a look that could only be described as contained excitement. "Yeah?"

I nodded, brushing the head of his cock over my clit. "Yeah."

But Colin was nothing if not thorough. "I'm clean…haven't been with anyone in months." He leaned down, pressing his lips to mine and lining himself up. Slipping the tip of his cock inside me at the same time his tongue met mine. He teased me relentlessly, inching in and out with the smallest of movements. Kissing me deeper until I was a writhing, moaning mess beneath him.

"Colin, please," I whispered as I finally tore my mouth from his.

"Fuck, I've dreamed of being bare inside this tight little pussy."

He pounded home over and over again, making me slide across the top of his desk, the first and only man ever to have entered me without a veil of latex between us, and I let go. All my fears, my worries, my hesitation when it came to Colin—I released it. He could have me any way he wanted, whether it was just for a few weekends as we worked on this project or for longer. I wanted him, and I would take what I could get. For now.

# chapter five

COLIN

THE DAYS HAD BEGUN running together since Sloane had started staying with me. I no longer remembered them by their titles, but rather in terms of what we'd done. Monday was sixty-nine in the library; Tuesday was ice play in the kitchen; Wednesday was blow job under my desk. If I had a different sexual situation every day for the rest of my life, I'd be perfectly fucking happy.

Today, the day before Christmas Eve—also known as woke Sloane with my tongue in her pussy—the estate was almost eerie in its silence. The full staff I'd hired for the mansion were off with their families, and the additional employees working on the mixed-use facility were on vacation until after the new year. Which meant it was just Sloane and me.

Exactly what I wanted.

I checked my phone to verify our evening plans before glancing at my watch. We needed to leave in thirty minutes to make it to Silver Quarter Farm by the designated time I'd set up with Grady. Recalling something Sloane had said months prior about her love for horses, I'd called in a favor to arrange for exclusive use of the property. Grady wasn't too happy about it. Though, to be fair, I hadn't found anything he was happy about at all in the years I'd known him.

After shutting off my laptop, I walked across the hall to Sloane's office. There she sat, her hair pulled back in a bun, sexy as hell glasses perched on her nose. She still wore her suit jacket, beneath it a bright red camisole I knew to be nearly as soft as her skin. I knew because I'd slipped it off her this morning as soon as she'd put it on and then dragged her back to bed.

She stared at something on her laptop, pen bouncing on her full lower lip. It was the same sight I'd seen a hundred times before, and it never failed to turn me on. In everything she did, she commanded the room, and it was hot as fuck. Especially when she relinquished that control in the bedroom.

I leaned against the doorjamb, my hands in my pockets, suit jacket hanging over my forearm. "Didn't you get the memo, Ms. McLaren?"

Her head shot up, her lips parted in surprise. She did a quick scan of me, letting her eyes drop to take in every inch. Many inches perked up when her gaze rested near my zipper. Then she met my eyes. "What memo?"

"It's quitting time."

"Colin." There was a note of exasperation in her tone. "It's barely six o'clock."

"I know you're going to find this hard to believe, but in most places, five is actually when people call it a day."

"Your office has never worked on the same rules as most places."

"Your dedication is duly noted and will be reflected in your next review. Now finish up and get your sweet ass over here. I want to take you somewhere."

"But…" Her brows drew down. "I thought George was off for the holiday."

"He is. I do know how to drive, spitfire. I think I can manage it."

"Fine. But I'm working tomorrow whether you like it or not. We still don't have steel at the port." She stood, smoothing her skirt as she walked toward me…didn't stop until she pressed her soft curves against me. Jesus, I wanted to fuck her against the doorway. Wanted to say screw the plans, no matter the thousands of dollars I'd spent on the evening, just so I could get inside her pussy. Again.

"Do I at least have time to change?"

I reached down and gripped her ass, hauling her up even higher than she stood in those hot-as-hell heels. With a hand cupping the back of her head, I kissed her, sliding my tongue against hers without preamble. Groaning when she met me stroke for stroke. Groaning even louder when her moan got lost in my mouth.

I finally forced myself to pull back. "You can change. Just wear panties you won't mind me ripping off later."

"Always so demanding."

"You love it."

Though she didn't respond, her answering smile said everything I needed to hear.

———

Sloane wasn't good with surprises. That much was clear as we traversed the short route to the northern tip of the island. Though that wasn't a shock. She liked being in control and was no doubt feeling itchy as she sat in the passenger's seat. She'd asked a dozen times where we were going. When I'd refused to tell her, she'd sent me a glare that would've had the balls of lesser men shriveling in their pants. Unfortunately for her, that glare had the opposite effect on me, my cock hard and begging for some of that aggression.

"Why can't you just tell me where we're going?"

"Why can't you just sit there, look pretty, and wait for me to show you?"

"Sit still and look pretty isn't really my style."

I slid her a look out of the corner of my eye. "Humor me."

Snow had begun to fall, just a light dusting but enough to make the drive take longer than planned. Even so, we were only five minutes away. And as far as I could tell from the crease between her brows, she had no idea where we were headed.

"You passed the bridge." She gestured out the window.

"I'm aware."

"If we're not going into the city, where are we headed? There's hardly any island left, unless your intention is to drive us into the lake."

"Jesus, woman. Would you just wait for your Christmas present to come into view?"

She spun toward me, her eyes bright. "You got me a present?"

"Yes. Now stop ruining it." I brought our clasped hands to my mouth and pressed a kiss against her hand.

Now that she knew this was her present, her excitement was palpable, her gaze darting around as she tried to puzzle out where we were going.

When I pulled off on the winding road that led to Grady's farm, her eyes widened, her gaze catching the large sign proclaiming Silver Quarter Farm. "You're taking me to…a horse farm?"

I glanced over as I entered the code on the gate, hoping the tone present in her voice was awe and not disgust. An evening at a farm wasn't a typical gift, but then again, Sloane wasn't a typical woman. "Not just any farm. The only Foundation Quarter Horse breeder in the state. There are stallions with Oklahoma Star and Three Bars lineage in that barn." Once the gates opened, I drove us another quarter mile down the path toward where Grady would be waiting. "They should have everything set up and ready for us."

"How…" She shook her head. "Colin, how did you manage this? I didn't even know there were horses on the island."

"Good thing you have me along, then." I shot her a wink as I pulled up and parked, glimpsing Grady and another man standing next to a horse-drawn carriage piled high with blankets, the canopy strung with twinkling white lights.

"It's beautiful," she breathed, then the men caught her attention. "Who're they?"

"The grumpy fuck on the right is Grady Drake, owner of the horse farm and the guy I sold my balls to to make this happen."

"Really?" She reached over to rub my cock through my pants, sassy smile on her face. My feisty girl. "Huh, they certainly seem to be attached."

"If you want to go on the tour and the carriage ride, you'd better stop." I held her hand against my quickly hardening cock. "Otherwise, I can't be held responsible for what I do. Even if they're watching."

"Fine." She leaned over and kissed me. "But I'm going to want to get up close and personal later. Make sure your balls are still intact."

"I would expect nothing less." Once out of the car, I strolled to her side, offering my hand to help her out. With her tucked into my side to absorb some of the chill of the night, we walked the short distance to where the two men were standing.

"You're late." Grady stood with his arms crossed, just a flannel covering his upper body. Apparently, the cold didn't affect jackasses. Between his plaid shirt and his full beard, he looked more like a lumberjack than a billionaire.

I shrugged. "You get paid either way."

"Paid, yes. Standing out here in the cold, I'm not fond of." He glanced at Sloane, a move that had me pulling her closer. "So you're the infamous Sloane McLaren."

"I'm not sure I'd go with infamous, but yes. I'm Sloane."

"I pictured you as some intellectual type. Can't be too smart if you're hooked up with this asshole."

I checked my watch. "Not even two minutes, and I already want to strangle you. I think that's a record."

"So, you two have a really warm relationship, then," Sloane said. "How'd you meet, anyway?"

"We own a resort in the Caribbean with another partner. Grady's the one who told me about the mall property for sale."

"And now that we've gone down memory lane, are you ready to get this evening started?" Grady asked. "My balls are about to shrivel up from the cold."

I leaned closer to Sloane, not bothering to lower my voice. "It's past his bedtime, so he's exceptionally pissy. But if you want to ask him anything about running the farm, he's happy to answer."

"I said I'd answer three questions. Three."

"For as much as I'm paying you, you should write her a damn book."

"For as much of my time as you're taking up, you should—"

"Okay, boys." Sloane patted my chest as she looked at Grady. "I appreciate the offer, and I'd love to take you up on that. May I email you after the new year? Give myself time to think about what I want to ask."

Grady grunted. "Fine."

The other man standing off to the side cleared his throat, getting our attention. "If you're ready, sir, I'll be your coachman this evening. I've got everything you requested prepared and in the carriage."

I squeezed Sloane's hip. "You ready?"

"Of course." She nodded to Grady. "It was nice to meet you. I look forward to speaking with you again."

Without another glance to Grady, I led Sloane to the carriage and held her hand as she climbed inside. Waiting for us was exactly what I'd requested—lots of blankets, spiked hot chocolate, and extra mittens and a hat in case Sloane hadn't brought hers.

I grabbed one of the thermoses and handed it to her before taking mine and settling back in the seat, my arm across her shoulders. "Can't have a carriage ride without hot chocolate." I brought my lips to her ear. "Plus a little something extra to make sure I get lucky tonight."

She tilted her head back, her smile lighting up her whole face. "I never realized that wasn't a sure thing."

"I didn't become a billionaire by counting on a sure thing."

It was a perfect night for this—the temperature hovered at thirty degrees, making it comfortable under all our gear and blankets. Snow fell softly, giving the whole ride an ethereal quality I couldn't have paid for. And then there was the company. Sloane's interest never waned as the coachman took us down several paths, pointing out the stables we'd tour later. After a while, he brought us to the edge of the property—a high point that overlooked the lake—and then took his leave to give us a bit of privacy.

I pulled Sloane into my side as she stared at the view, mouth parted. Resting my lips against her temple, I asked, "So how'd I do on the whole Christmas present thing?"

She shook her head, then looked up at me. "Amazing. I can't believe you did all this."

I shrugged. Honestly, I wished I could've done more. "You mentioned how much you loved horseback rides. I know there's a little more snow than you're used to, but I wanted to make sure you spent the holiday happy since you're stuck here with me."

"I wouldn't say stuck." She slid her hand inside my coat, resting it over my stomach. "I can't believe you remembered what I said. That was...what? My first week on the island? You asked my holiday plans, and I was feeling nostalgic. I assumed you'd forgotten."

"From anyone else, I probably would've."

She hugged me closer, and I couldn't resist anymore. I leaned down and kissed her, letting my hand slip under the wool coat and sweater she wore. Wanting to strip her down right there or take her home and have my way with her. But there was more in store, and I wanted her to experience it all.

After the coachman took us back to the stables, we toured the farm by foot, Sloane's eyes lighting up with every new thing revealed. Her entire demeanor changed—going from in-charge, hardass Sloane to inquisitive, excited Sloane. Both were amazing, but she seemed so happy here. I loved the other part of her, the commanding version I saw in the office, but there was something to be said about this softer side of her. Something I wanted to see a lot more of.

But Sloane was a contracted employee, only with me until the mixed-use facility was complete. And then she'd be on her way to other projects, kicking ass and taking names.

The problem was, I wanted her by my side for the foreseeable future—not just working for me, but being with me.

And, if I was honest with myself, I wanted her for the not-so-foreseeable future, too. I wanted her as long as she'd have me.

# chapter six



"COLIN."

"Sloane." His muffled voice brought with it a puff of hot air right over my clit. What a way to wake up.

But I had things to do, emails to send, calls to return. There was no time for his attentions. "Colin, while I appreciate what you're—"

I couldn't finish, my brain short-circuiting as he spread my lips and suckled my clit. I threw back the covers so I could see him, needing to find his eyes, but he wasn't looking at me. No, he was focused completely on the task at hand—on loving my pussy with his mouth as he'd done every day since we'd started this…thing. This thing that had quickly turned from hate-fucking to something on the other end of the emotional spectrum. Something sweet and soft that made my heart squeeze when I thought about it. Something I wasn't ready to put a name to yet.

As Colin lapped at me, spreadsheets, conference calls, and shipment logs danced through my head—all things I needed to finish before we officially broke for Christmas. I also needed to find time to go back to the B&B where I'd definitely not been staying the past week to grab more clothes and Colin's Christmas present. I fisted his hair, my brain ready to push him off as my task list built, but my body overrode the directive. Colin was too good at what he was doing, and he made me want to forget everything except the feel of his tongue and hands.

I was helpless to resist.

Instead of pushing, I yanked him closer, loving how he growled against my skin. How he clenched my thighs tighter. He reared up like a beast, dragging me with him until my hips were off the bed and he held me up. Licking me from one end to the other and making me tremble. I couldn't take myself away from him just yet. It'd be cruel...to both of us.

"Five minutes." I tugged his hair and let my legs fall open a little wider. "You've got five minutes, then I need to get to work."

Colin chuckled and pulled away, his eyes bright as they met mine, his stubbled cheek rough against my inner thigh. "Your boss is a real asshole to make you work on Christmas Eve."

"Tell me about it. But the benefits are good."

I cupped his face, running a thumb over his lips, knowing the wetness all over them was from me.

"Just good?" He dropped me down to the mattress, holding my gaze as he opened his mouth and sucked my clit between his lips. Such a filthy image, so damned obscene. And I loved it. I arched and squirmed, knowing he wouldn't need the full five minutes to get me off. Not when he was so intent on watching me fall apart. He was too good at this, too skilled. And I was a lucky, lucky woman.

"Fine. The benefits are amazing." I groaned and grabbed his hair again, throwing my head back as he slid two fingers inside me. "They're awesome. Tremendous. There are no benefits better. Now please, don't stop."

He definitely didn't stop.

———

While Colin showered close to an hour later—he may not have needed the extra time, but he deserved it with me riding him until he'd groaned my name—I threw on a pair of yoga pants and a shirt, grabbed my phone to check my emails, and headed downstairs. The house was empty other than Colin and me. There was no need for propriety; I could've worked naked, and Colin wouldn't have cared. Well, he'd have cared. Enough to probably fuck me from one side of my office to the other. That couldn't happen, though. I needed to get my tasks done so we could celebrate Christmas Eve properly. With eggnog and sex under the Christmas tree. Lots of sex under the tree, and in front of the fireplace, and maybe—

One email stopped me in my tracks, the subject line enough to make my blood run cold.

Steel Shipment Not Yet Released—Unsure of Production Schedule Before Chinese New Year

"Fuck." I practically ran to my office, lunging for my laptop. The steel we needed for the mall project, the conference call where we hadn't pinned down Frank about final dates because I'd—

"No, no, no, this can't be happening."

But it was. Frank's email laid out the problems with the factory, the not knowing if he could persuade them to speed up production for us, and the lack of direction after the last conference call on what we were willing to do to solve the issue.

Lack. Of. Direction.

That was one hundred percent my fault. I'd blanked out on the call because I'd dropped to my knees for Colin. I'd been distracted and focused on sex instead of work all week. I'd expected my team to follow up with Frank and me, but I hadn't explicitly told them to, and now they were all gone for the holiday. I'd dropped the ball, something that never happened to me. Though I never slept with my boss, so...

"You snuck down without me." Colin sauntered into the room looking clean-shaven and well-rested.

And happy enough to make my stomach drop with dread. "I thought you might've joined me in the shower."

"No time." I tore my eyes away from him to focus on my screen, already calculating time zones and a normal person's schedule. Would Frank still be awake? It was a possibility, which meant I needed to get on the phone. And whether Frank was available or not, I needed to stay away from Colin right then. I had to focus on work. "I have too much to do this morning for playing, Colin. Maybe I can swing by your office for lunch."

He stood silent for a long moment, the tension in the room rising. This wasn't what we did anymore; that wasn't how I spoke to him. Not since we'd started this…thing. Not since I'd started to fall for him. But I'd just screwed up so badly, he'd lose more money than I could imagine. Badly enough I doubted my career would survive if word got out. I had no time to be in love with my boss, a thought that both felt so right and made me want to cry.

It was time to get back to business.

"Please, Colin." I huffed, making sure my business mask was firmly in place before looking up at his confused face. "I need to do my job."

He nodded, his eyes narrowed in a way that told me he didn't buy my line. "Fine. But it's Christmas Eve. You're not working late."

My smile felt plastic and fake. "Let's regroup in a few hours and see where we're at."

I went back to my computer, waiting for him to leave. For the pressure on my chest to ease. When he finally left after not saying another word to me, I sighed and shook my head. Christmas Eve? I had a feeling I'd be working all Christmas Day, probably in another country, one that didn't celebrate the holiday and would be in full work mode. But there was too much to do before I made that decision. I grabbed my phone and dialed the number for Frank, crossing my fingers he'd pick up. Jumping in the second I heard the phone click, not waiting for his greeting.

"Frank, it's Sloane McLaren. We need to talk about the steel shipment."

## COLIN

———

Jesus, she was magnificent when she worked, all focused intensity packed into the body I knew nearly better than my own. Didn't matter if she wore a suit or yoga pants and T-shirt, she exuded power. And it made me hard as a fucking rock.

But she wasn't in the mood for playing. She'd made that much perfectly clear.

Every time I'd glanced in at her, hard at work, brow pinched as she tried to figure something out, I had to remind myself this was what I'd hired her for.

She was the best in the whole goddamn country, and she'd proven that every day.

She was proving it now, even when I didn't want her to.

Whenever I'd slipped into her office, she'd shooed me away, either with her words or actually shoving me out from behind her desk. It was totally unexpected… and new for me. I never got distracted at work. I never allowed myself to be. Yet Sloane did that to me. I couldn't concentrate on anything knowing she was in the next room, driving me crazy. Thank God I had her to keep things running smoothly, because I certainly wasn't in the mind-space to do so.

After multiple unsuccessful attempts to distract her, I decided to go to the residential wing and make some calls. She could work during Christmas Eve day, but I was going to spoil her rotten tonight. The long corridors were quiet and empty, even though they were full of furniture. Furniture that no doubt cost a fortune but was just pieces someone had picked out to fill the space. It never used to bother me, being alone in this huge mansion while Sloane had gone back to the bed-and-breakfast, but after only eight days, it was already hard to remember how I'd survived.

I wanted the life Sloane brought to this oversized estate. I wanted the arguments and the pushback and the laughter and the fun. I wanted everything she had to give.

I just needed to figure out how the hell to tell her.

We only had a few more months left on the

mixed-use facility project, and then she'd be gone. Back to Colorado before her next assignment. And I had no projects in the pipeline with which to entice her to stay.

Looked like I had to rely on charm and charisma.

Sloane's scent infiltrated my bedroom, touches of her everywhere. She'd made a trip to the B&B to gather a few changes of clothes once it'd become apparent I wasn't going to let her sleep anywhere but my bed. They hung in my closet next to my suits. Her brush sat on the counter in the bathroom, the bottle of water she needed every night perched on her nightstand next to her Kindle she'd not once had time to open. If she was in bed, she was either asleep or riding my cock.

"Jesus." I reached down and adjusted myself, considering slipping into the shower and getting a little relief, but quickly dismissing the thought. I still needed to make some calls to get things set up for this evening.

First call was to Antonio Ricci, owner of Nonno Pino's. The little Italian restaurant was the nicest on the island, the food spectacular. It'd be the perfect place for tonight. Once the restaurant was secured for our exclusive use, I dialed The Bloom Room to order some arrangements to be brought there. The atmosphere at Nonno Pino's was nice, but I didn't want nice. I wanted the best.

Three hours later, everything was set up. Hopefully, Sloane had been able to get done what she needed to, because she wasn't working this evening. Our reservations were for seven, and the boxes of clothing possibilities would arrive around five. I'd broken the cardinal rule and peeked at the size of Sloane's suits so I could have my personal shopper send over a few dresses and accessories for her to try on. My only stipulation? Every single one had to be red.

Fuck, the thought of Sloane in a red dress, lips the same color, eyes dark and wanting, made me ache all over. I wasn't sure I'd be able to wait hours for dinner.

Knowing I needed to get out of the house if I had any hopes of letting her get work done, I shot Sloane a quick text to let her know I was leaving and grabbed my keys. I hadn't checked the progress of the site since the last time Sloane and I'd stopped by, and I wanted to see what they'd been able to accomplish in a week.

Not allowing myself to even peek into her office, I headed straight for my Mercedes. Counting down the hours until dinner.

# chapter seven



THREE HOURS, TWELVE CALLS, and a couple of panicked emails later, I was screwed. Colin was screwed. The entire mall project was screwed. I'd dropped the ball, and there was only one way I could see to possibly keep the project moving on target so Colin didn't lose hundreds of thousands of dollars as his crews sat idle.

I needed to fly to China. Immediately.

But first, I had one more call to make. One favor to ask. I dialed hesitantly, knowing there was a chance my one true friend in the industry wouldn't be able to help. But I had to try.

"Jane Hatfield." Her voice was as clipped as ever, her words direct. No soft, friendly greeting like one might expect.

"It's Sloane McLaren. I have a proposition for you."

"I don't even get a hello? A how you doing? Straight to business for the first call you've blessed me with in weeks?"

"Jane." I closed my eyes and took a deep breath. "I screwed up, and I need your help to fix it."

There was a pause, a longer silence than I'd been prepared for, but Jane never disappointed. "Is the screw-up business or personal?"

"Both."

"Fucking A, Sloane." The sound of a door closing came through the line. "What did you do? Tell me you didn't sleep with your boss?"

Yep, no bullshit from Jane. "I—"

"You did. You motherfucking did. Number one rule of being a woman in this industry is don't fuck the boss. You taught me that after the whole Robinson debacle, and now here you are, needing me to save your hide. Talk about turning full circle."

"I know. Trust me, I know. But I can't take it back." Colin's sleepy smile came to mind, memories of his hand holding mine on our carriage ride. His sweet words late at night when we were alone in bed and close to sleep. "I wouldn't want to."

"Oh, Sloane. Did you fall for him?"

My answer was immediate and sincere. "Yes, I did. Completely."

"Then you're a bigger idiot than I thought."

"Jane, please." I took a deep breath, trying hard to ignore her judgment. Jane had a right to be bitter, but Colin wasn't Robinson. Not by a long shot.

"You're the only person I can trust to handle this. I need your help."

Jane fell silent, and when she spoke again, her voice was nowhere near as firm. "It's Christmas Eve."

"I know, and you live an hour away from where the job is stationed."

"Where's that?"

"Temperance Falls. The island. Do you know it?"

Jane huffed a sarcastic sort of snort. "Everyone around here knows it."

"Will you come?"

"I'm already packing."

I threw my fist in the air, biting back a whoop as I tried to stay calm and professional. "I'll email you the address and project details." Colin's smile danced in front of my memories again, making my stomach clench with something akin to guilt and stealing away the relief I felt at Jane's acceptance. He was going to hate me. "And Jane?"

"Yeah?"

I hated doubting Colin's focus, but I had to make sure she understood. He'd need kid gloves for a bit, someone to put up with him. "He's going to be cranky I left, but I have to get on a plane to save the project. Try not to push him too hard."

Jane snorted. "Fine. I'll baby your lover's sour mood while you're away."

"One last thing—"

"What? What now?"

I lowered my voice, sincerity my only goal. "Thank you."

"You owe me."

"I do. I really do."

"Go save the world, McLaren. I'll pick up the pieces you leave behind. Merry fucking Christmas."

When she hung up, I stared at my phone for a good minute, trying to see a way to explain this to Colin without him telling me I didn't need to go. He wouldn't like it, wouldn't want me in China and away from him, especially for Christmas, but this was for the best. I couldn't do my job while spending so much time in his bed, which meant things needed to change. I had goals and dreams to be met, and he had a project he'd invested a fortune into. The timing was wrong for us, that was all.

But timing was everything in my world, and holidays were often missed.

Within five minutes, I had a flight, a hotel, and a plan in place to keep the project on track. I'd need to borrow Colin's private jet, the one sitting at the Temperance Falls airport, to get to an international airport, but he'd understand. Thankfully, the pilot was easily reached and said he could be ready in time. I didn't ask him not to tell Colin because that felt dishonest, but I certainly hoped he'd keep my plans to himself until we were in the air. I'd flown with him a number of times before without issue—I assumed this would appear like any other situation to him.

Travel plans locked in, I moved quickly through

my last tasks so I'd have time to swing by my place and grab my jump bag. I typed up notes for Jane, set up an admin access for her on my office computer, and did everything I could to make the transition smooth from me to her.

Taking the time I felt the final task deserved, I handwrote a letter, wanting something personal to leave for Colin. Needing him to know I took the time to really think about him before I left. Not that those thoughts would dissuade me.

When everything was complete, I looked over my desk. Double-checking I wasn't forgetting anything. I'd made sure Business Colin wouldn't be too inconvenienced by my departure by hiring Jane and making sure all the pieces of his enterprise would keep moving as expected. Business Colin would be fine. Personal Colin? The man I'd been slowly falling in love with over the past two weeks?

I didn't know if he'd ever forgive me.

## COLIN

———

THE PROGRESS AT THE mixed-use facility was much slower than I wanted—than was necessary. So much of what the contractors could do hinged on the arrival of the steel needed to be able to move forward with the upper-level build—where the compact, affordable apartments for the residents of Temperance Falls would be. We'd be offering single- or double-sized, the smaller perfect for a college student or a recent graduate, or even an executive working on the island for a limited amount of time. The double units would be available for anyone seeking a bit more space.

I needed an update from Sloane on when the steel would be arriving and adjust for any timing delays, should that be necessary. I was paying a pretty penny to get this fast-tracked. We'd already sold several units on blueprints alone, and I would not allow their move-in dates to be pushed back. That wasn't the kind of business I ran.

Those thoughts were pushed to the back of my head when I spotted a sleek Lexus SUV in front of the mansion—Marla, the personal shopper I'd hired while on the island. Thank fuck I'd had the foresight to keep her on retainer in the event I'd need her at the drop of a hat. When she was getting paid as much as she was, she had no problem taking a quick drive to the island from the city with thousands of dollars of clothing in her trunk.

"Special evening planned?" she asked as she stepped from her car. She smiled, her hand outstretched to greet me. Her blond hair, streaked with gray, was pulled back into a tight bun, the laugh lines around her face showing a life well lived.

"Just dinner." I shook her hand before moving to take the boxes from the back of her car.

"Mhmm…" She shot me a smile as she grabbed

a couple shopping bags, then hit a button on her key fob to close the back end. "Well, whoever the lovely lady is, she's a lucky woman. What I wouldn't give to have Stanley surprise me with an evening out and have enough thought to get me clothing options… It's so romantic."

"Well, tell your husband to up his game, then. That poor bastard's going to lose the best thing that ever happened to him if he doesn't watch it."

She laughed, shaking her head as she followed me inside. The office wing was on the other side of the estate, so I wasn't concerned with Sloane hearing us.

"You can just set the bags down over there. I'll get them brought up to my room."

"Of course. And you let me know how it all goes. Give me a call, and I'll swing by to pick up the pieces she didn't care for—if there are any, of course." With a wink and a smile, she left, waving over her shoulder as she closed the front door behind her.

After running the boxes and shopping bags up to my bedroom, I made my way to the office wing. It was after five, but I should've known I'd have to pry Sloane from her desk. God knew she wouldn't leave willingly. The hallway was silent, not even the tapping of her fingers on the keyboard of her laptop. Actually, everything was silent. The house was positively still.

The lamp on her desk illuminated the room enough so I could see she wasn't in it. She hadn't been upstairs, either. And the kitchen had been dark on my way down. Where the hell was she?

I walked into the space, going to her desk to see if she'd left her iPad behind—it was her lifeline, and she wouldn't go anywhere without it. But it was gone. Instead, a lone piece of paper, folded once, sat in the middle of her desk. I picked it up and unfolded it, my brow creasing as I read.

*Colin,*

*I failed at following up on the steel shipment, which could delay the entire build. I take complete responsibility for my error and fully intend to correct it. I've brought on a trusted associate to manage the project from Temperance Falls while I head to China to sort out the manufacturing issues. Her name is Jane, and she should be at the mansion before the end of the evening.*

*I care deeply for you, but our personal relationship cannot affect our professional one. Due to the changes in our situation, I feel it is only appropriate that I terminate our agreement effective the moment I verify the steel is on the water.*

*Sincerely,*
*Sloane McLaren*

Oh, fuck no. She thought because she made a mistake—true, a mistake that could cost hundreds of thousands of dollars, but a mistake nonetheless—she not only couldn't work for me, but she couldn't be with me anymore?

I pulled out my phone and dialed my pilot, even as I hurried out of the mansion and to my car.

"Good evening, Mr. Huntley. What can I do for you?" he asked. "I've got Ms. McLaren scheduled to leave in fifteen."

"If you want to keep your job, the wheels of that jet don't leave the runway before I get there. I'm on my way."

I didn't wait for his response before ending the call and tossing my phone in the passenger's seat, speeding my way toward Temperance Falls airport. If Sloane thought she was involved with the kind of man who sat around and let things happen to him, she hadn't been paying attention.

I fought for what I wanted. And I always, always got it.

# chapter eight

SLOANE

COLIN'S PRIVATE JET SAT on the runway, silent and still as the pilot ran through his safety checklists out in the lightly falling snow. The cabin was quiet and warm, bright against the gloomy sky, making it easy to fall into work. I needed to keep my mind off the mistake I'd made—off how disappointed Colin would be—and focus on fixing everything. I emailed several Chinese contacts from my phone, setting up my visit. There was leverage to use, history of money spent, and the potential for future orders to threaten with. The steel had to be on the water before Chinese New Year, or we'd lose more than a month. We'd be cutting it close even with me there monitoring everything. I could've kicked myself for losing over a week of work time because of a distraction.

A sexy, sweet, amazing distraction who might never forgive me, but a distraction nonetheless.

I wasn't paying attention to the comings and goings of the pilot or airport crew—wasn't aware of anything but the plans playing out in my head, the virtual GANTT chart happening behind my eyes—until someone sat beside me.

Colin.

Still as stone, he stared straight ahead. Barely even breathing. My heart raced, and my stomach bottomed out as I inspected him quickly, sizing him up.

He looked pissed.

"Colin, I—"

"A trip to China is going to make it difficult to get to our seven o'clock reservation." Words clipped, tone dark. Definitely pissed.

"I didn't know we had a reservation."

He finally looked my way, those stunning hazel eyes holding mine and refusing to let go. "I didn't know we had a trip to China on the schedule."

"We don't, but I need to fix the mistake I made. That requires me to be in China."

"And instead of coming to me and us making a decision on how best to proceed, you decided to go on without my input."

And right there was the problem. Personal life overlapping business. Two weeks ago, he would've praised me for getting the job done no matter what. Now...not so much. "Our personal relationship would have influenced the business decisions you needed to make."

He let out a breath, looking irritated. "You're not giving me a whole lot of credit, Sloane. I didn't get where I am by making stupid decisions."

"Would you have told me to go? Knowing that the entire build would be held up if someone didn't take over and get the job done? Would you have put me on a plane to fix this? Even though I'd miss Christmas with you?"

"If that's what needs to be done, yes."

He laid his hand on his knee, palm side up. I had this vision of teenagers in a movie theater, of a young man sending a signal and giving the girl with him a chance to respond. That hand was Colin's move, and he waited to see if I'd respond.

I slid my hand into his without so much as a blink, making his lips turn up the slightest bit.

"But," he said as he wove our fingers together. "I'd put you on the plane knowing you'd come back to me."

"I am coming back to you."

"And yet your resignation letter says you're not."

Oh. He thought…no wonder he looked mad. He was hiding his hurt. I reached for him, cupping the side of his face and running my thumb over his stubble. "I resigned the job, not the relationship."

He leaned into my hand, turning to kiss my palm. "What if I said I wanted both?"

"We can't work together, Colin. I've quite possibly cost you enough money to buy a fleet of yachts because I was too busy blowing you to do my job. That's a problem."

"It's not ideal, I'll give you that. But I don't throw out a good thing and start all over when problems arise. I've never run my business that way—that should be clear to you by now. Why would you think this was any different?" He lifted our joined hands, kissing the back of mine softly. "Especially this."

"Colin, I want this, too… But it won't work if I'm more of a detriment to a client than not. I'd never forgive myself if I made a mistake that cost you money, that kept your crews from working and getting paid. I won't destroy your business and my reputation when I know stepping away would be a better option."

"Sloane, you're the best Operations VP I've ever hired, and this one hiccup doesn't change that." He took a deep breath, grabbing my other hand so he held both. "I've negotiated with you once, and I'm ready to do it again. So tell me what it'll take to make sure I get to keep my hot-as-hell spitfire in my bed every night, and the take-no-prisoners Sloane in my office every day." Colin leaned in to nip my bottom lip, sending a shiver up my spine. "I want to see those sexy legs taunting me under your desk before they're wrapped around my head in our bedroom."

I bit back a smile. "Be serious."

His eyebrows went up, his face totally deadpan. "I never joke about your legs."

But the humor only lasted so long, and reality

found a way of creeping back into our romantic bubble. "I won't fail this project—I simply don't fail. I also won't put myself in a position where that's a high risk. I want you, Colin, but I don't think I should be your Vice President of Operations anymore."

He blew out a breath and stroked my wrist with his thumb. "You know I want you. And you know I'm greedy. I want you in my bed and in my office. We can make it work. Even with this snag, I have complete faith in what you can do. Just promise me you won't make any decisions until you get back."

Before I could respond, the pilot stepped into the seating area. "Sorry to interrupt, but if Ms. McLaren is going to make her flight, we need to get in the air."

Colin's lips twisted into a frown. "Two minutes."

I kept my eyes on his, leaning closer as the pilot stepped outside. Pressing my lips to his just once. "I have to go. I need to fix this."

"You will fix this. It's what you do." He wrapped his arms around me, pulling me across the seat and onto his lap. "You're going to kick ass over there, and then you're going to come back to me so we can finish this discussion. Because I'm not giving up."

"So stubborn."

"It's how I get what I want." He brought his lips to mine again, this time taking us from sweet to hot and deep in a matter of seconds. His tongue slid against mine as he gripped my thighs. I shifted, moving to straddle him, to rub against him. This was it, our last few moments together before I flew off to the other side of the world for who knew how long. As much as we started out adversarial, our relationship had changed. Morphed into something else entirely. And being without him for these next few weeks—

"Going to miss you," I murmured as he dragged his mouth down my neck. "Going to miss this."

"Me too." He gripped my legs, pulling me closer. Rocking me against his hard cock. I fell into his rhythm without thought, breathing hard as he pulled us closer.

At least until the plane engines came to life.

We stopped moving, both staring. Both breathing hard. This was it—time to go. No more distractions.

"You should go back to the mansion." I slid off his lap and into my seat, wanting so badly to drag him with me. "I need to get to work."

I was expecting another fight, another discussion, but instead, Colin smiled in a sad sort of way and stood. "My bed's going to be awfully lonely while you're gone." He braced his hands on the arms of my seat and leaned down, close enough for me to feel his breath across my cheek. To practically feel his demand. "Be sure to schedule phone sex into your planner. And send nudes. Lots and lots of nudes."

Some sort of knot released inside me, the fear that he'd really stop me from doing my job because of our personal relationship. I should've known better, should've trusted. "You're ridiculous."

He gave me a sexy smile and one last sweet kiss before standing to his full height. "Call me when you land."

"Promise. I'll be back in a week or so."

He looked thoughtful for a moment. "I think one nude picture for every hour you're gone should suffice."

I laughed as he walked off the plane, watching him cut across the falling snow through the windows. I'd miss him, that was for sure. Miss his sweet side and his filthy side. But I had a job to do. I'd finish what I started with The Huntley Group, make sure their project went smoothly so there was no loss of money or work time, and then…

Then I'd come back and tell that man how much I loved him.

# chapter nine

COLIN

SLOANE HAD BEEN GONE for a week, but it felt like a lifetime. What kind of sad fuck did that make me? I'd never been someone who relied on other people to feel complete. Yet there was no denying something was missing with her gone.

I hadn't been alone since she'd left—she'd arranged for a colleague to take her place while she was in China. Direct and assertive, Jane knew how to get shit done, but she was a poor substitute for Sloane.

As it was New Year's Eve, I'd sent Jane home hours ago. I sat in the sitting area of my bedroom, glass of bourbon hanging from my fingers as I stared at the bed that no longer smelled like Sloane. I wanted her back, but she had a job to do. She'd sent me daily updates—she'd been able to get things back on track, just like I knew she could. Only loose ends had to be tied up, and then she'd be home sometime next week.

Too long.

We'd managed to work in a couple calls and even an X-rated Skype session, but it wasn't enough. This week without her confirmed what I'd begun to suspect: I was in love with her. Had been falling every day for the past six months, everything slotting into place when she'd finally surrendered to our attraction.

And I didn't want to be without her—in my business or personal life. We could find a way to make it work. I just had to convince her.

I set my glass down and leaned my head against the back of the oversized leather chair, closing my eyes. My phone rested on my knee, waiting for Sloane's call. It'd become a sort of unspoken agreement between us that she'd call before starting her day. Bonus that hers was the last voice I heard before going to bed.

"Drinking alone? That's not a good sign."

I snapped open my eyes, jerking my head up. She stood in the doorway in a tight skirt and camisole. Hair loose, lips quirked at the corners, looking hot as fuck—if tired.

If she didn't have those circles under her eyes, I'd swear she was a mirage. She'd told me she wouldn't be back for another week, and now she stood in my bedroom. I shook my head, finally finding my voice. "It's New Year's Eve, and the woman I want to ring in the new year with is halfway around the world. Or was supposed to be. You told me yesterday you still had things to do."

She shrugged and prowled toward me, hips swaying almost obscenely, my mouth watering as if on command. "I may have exaggerated a few things."

Once she reached me, I slid my hands up the back of her thighs, slipping beneath her skirt. Loving the feel of her silky skin against my fingertips. "How many things?"

Leaning forward, she ran her hands down my chest, her fingers slowly trailing all the way down to my waistband, almost greedy in their exploration. As if she'd been as miserable this week without me as I had been without her. "The steel went through customs without a hitch. I stayed just long enough to watch the ship set sail, and then I headed for the airport."

"I see." I cupped her ass, tugging her forward, my cock already hard as stone. "So the only thing you exaggerated was the fact that you weren't coming home for a while, is that right?"

"That. And perhaps a few of the challenges over there. Once I fired Frank, everything ran smoothly." She undid my pants, opening them wide to trace around my erection with a light touch. "By the way, I fired Frank."

I hummed, the subtle pressure on my cock not nearly enough to satisfy. Not after a week without her. "So you went over there and started kicking ass and taking names, just like I knew you would." Once I stripped her of her skirt and panties, I kissed her hip bones as she peeled off her camisole. And then finally, finally, she stood naked before me. "Never had a doubt you could pull this off."

"Speaking of pulling off…" She tugged at my shirt, eyes hooded with want.

With a growl, I stood, gripping her by the ass and hauling her to the bed. My clothes flew off in a frenzy, and then I was on top of her, settling between her legs and sliding into the most perfect heaven I'd ever known.

"Jesus, I missed this. Missed you." I hitched her knee over my hip, opening her wider for me. Allowing me to slide as deep as we both needed.

"Missed you so much." She arched under me, her breasts pointing straight to my mouth. I sucked one tip between my lips, flicking it with my tongue, loving the taste of her. Loving even more how she gripped my hair and begged, "Don't stop. Please don't stop."

"Never," I promised, thrusting harder and faster while pressing my thumb to her clit, desperate to get her to the edge with me.

After a week of nothing but self-loving, it didn't take long for either of us to reach our peaks. At the first pulse of her pussy around my cock, my name on her lips, I finally let myself go, groaning into her mouth as I spilled inside her.

Spent and sated, I kissed a path down her neck

while she traced soft circles along my back. Not realizing until that moment how much I'd missed not only the sex, but also the quiet moments between us. Moments like this. It was…perfection, and I wanted it. Every bit of it—the business talk and the amazing sex and the togetherness. I wanted it all with her.

I rolled to the side, pulling her to face me. Needing to find out if she was in this with me. "Did you think more about my proposition?"

She nodded. "I did—I had a lot of time alone to think about it."

"Do I need to start the next round of negotiations while I fuck you again, or did you find my suggestions satisfactory?"

"I don't need negotiations, just clarification."

I reached out, brushing the hair away from her face. Running my thumb over her bottom lip. Already hardening again. So fucking hungry for her. "Let me make this clear: I want you to work for me, permanently. No more contracts. During the day, you kick ass being my right-hand woman. In the evening, you're in my bed—our bed. Every night."

She stared at me with something that looked an awful lot like hope. "You're sure you're ready for that? Me…us…twenty-four seven?"

"Well, you are a handful, but I think I'm man enough for the challenge."

"Be serious."

I gripped her ass, pulling her closer as I brushed

a kiss against her lips. "Spitfire…I want you with me. As much as I can get. Don't tell anyone, but I was miserable while you were gone."

She bit her lip, a smile stretching her mouth. "Really?"

"A sad, miserable bastard. Before you showed up, I was moping about how my sheets didn't smell like you any longer. That's the kind of man you've reduced me to."

"Mind your words—I'm quite fond of that man."

"Are you now?"

"Yes." With a hand against my chest, she pushed me to my back and straddled me, sliding her pussy along my cock. "Arrogant attitude, demanding nature, and overbearing jackassery aside…I'm in love with him."

Relief flooded me as I cupped her neck and pulled her down, kissing the smile on her lips. "You fell in love with an asshole like that, huh?"

"Completely."

I ran my thumb along her jaw, my eyes connected with hers. Making sure she knew this wasn't a game. That these weren't just words. "Good, because he loves you, too."

Her smile lit up her whole face as she reached down to guide me between her legs. And as much as I wanted that, wanted to slide inside that tight, wet paradise, I needed an answer first. I gripped her hips, not letting her sink down on me.

"What is it?"

"Put me out of my misery and tell me you'll move in with me. We can live anywhere you want. I'll even buy us a horse farm if that'll make you happy. So long as you're in my bed every night."

She rested her lips against mine. "You drive a hard bargain, Huntley, but I accept." Pushing back, she slapped my hands out of the way and finally sank down, our moans mixing as I filled her again. "God, I've missed you."

"Me too." I raised my knees so she could rest back against them, opening her to my hungry gaze. Pink and swollen and glistening, clit peeking out, begging for my touch. "I've also missed your sweet pussy. A week is too long."

"Way too long." She tossed her head back, groaning as I fingered her clit, her pussy already fluttering around my cock.

I rocked up into her, keeping the pace slow and sweet until her orgasm took hold, sweeping her away, her body bowed back as she pulsed around me. All the while wondering how I got lucky enough to call this feisty, take-no-prisoners woman mine. Wondering if she'd ever know only a woman as strong as her could happily bring me to my knees.

Wondering how forever with her could possibly be long enough.

# Trouble is brewing in
# Temperance Falls

*The last thing a newly hired dean should be doing is one of his students...*

Dirty flirting with the unbelievably hot barista at Bundt & Grind café is not how Elliott Goodridge should be spending his time. Temperance Falls College hired him to counteract a scandal—not burn through his paychecks on overpriced coffee with a side of impure thoughts.

For the amount of time college student Samantha Monroe spends fantasizing about the new guy in town, she should know more than just his name. But despite putting out all kinds of signs that she's down for, well, putting out, Elliott hasn't made a move. Yet.

By the time the truth is revealed, it's too late to stop the charge between them. Sparks fly, but so do rumors. For Elliott, a day without his hands on Sam is too long—and two orgasm-free weeks until graduation is flat-out impossible.

# Seducing
# His Student

# about the author

London Hale is the combined pen name of writing besties Ellis Leigh and Brighton Walsh. Between them, they've published more than thirty books in the contemporary romance, paranormal romance, and romantic suspense genres. Ellis is a *USA Today* bestselling author who loves coffee, thinks green Skittles are the best, and prefers to stay in every weekend. Brighton is multi-published with Berkley, St. Martin's Press, and Carina Press. She hates coffee, thinks green Skittles are the work of the devil, and has never heard of a party she didn't want to attend. Don't ask how they became such good friends or work so well together—they still haven't figured it out themselves.

www.londonhale.com

www.ingramcontent.com/pod-product-compliance
Lightning Source LLC
Chambersburg PA
CBHW032049180726
48284CB00004B/1255